Join the fun on
Mudpuddle Farm

Pigs Might Fly

D1301600

Books by Michael Morpurgo

For younger readers:

MUDPUDDLE FARM: ALIEN INVASION!

MUDPUDDLE FARM: COCK-A-DOODLE-DOO!

MUDPUDDLE FARM: HEE-HAW HOORAY!

MUDPUDDLE FARM: PIGS MIGHT FLY!

COOL!

THE BUTTERFLY LION

THE FOX AND THE GHOST KING

MR. SKIP

For older readers:

BORN TO RUN

AN EAGLE IN THE SNOW

AN ELEPHANT IN THE GARDEN

KASPAR—PRINCE OF CATS

LISTEN TO THE MOON

LITTLE MANFRED

A MEDAL FOR LEROY

RUNNING WILD

SHADOW

michael morpurgo

Mudpuddle Farm

Pigs Might Fly

Illustrated by Shoo Rayner

HarperCollins *Children's Books*

And Pigs Might Fly first published in hardback by
A&C Black (Publishers) Limited 1983
First published in paperback by Collins, a division of
HarperCollins, 1988

Jigger's Day Off first published in hardback by
A&C Black (Publishers) Limited 1995
First published in paperback by Collins, a division of
HarperCollins, 1989

This bind-up edition first published in Great Britain by
HarperCollins *Children's Books* in 2008
First published in the United States of America in this edition by
HarperCollins *Children's Books* 2018
HarperCollins *Children's Books* is a division of
HarperCollins*Publishers* Ltd,
HarperCollins Publishers
1 London Bridge Street
London SE1 9GF

The HarperCollins website address is:
www.harpercollins.co.uk
1

Text copyright © Michael Morpurgo 1983, 1989
Illustrations copyright © Shoo Rayner 1983, 1989
All rights reserved.

ISBN 978–0–00–826909–8

Michael Morpurgo and Shoo Rayner assert the moral right to be identified as the
author and illustrator respectively of the work.

Printed and bound in Great Britain by CPI Group (UK) Ltd, Croydon CR0 4YY

Find out more about HarperCollins and the environment at
www.harpercollins.co.uk/green

Contents

And Pigs Might Fly

Chapter One

There was once a family of all kinds of animals that lived in the farmyard behind the tumbledown barn on Mudpuddle Farm.

At first light every morning Frederick, the flame-feathered rooster, lifted his eyes to the sun and crowed and crowed until the light came on in old Farmer Rafferty's bedroom window.

Ah, sweet mystery of light, at last I've found you...

One by one the animals crept out into

the dawn and stretched and yawned and

scratched themselves; but no one ever

spoke a word, not until after breakfast.

Old Farmer Rafferty put in his teeth,
looked out of his bathroom window
and shook his head.

And he opened the window and
shouted,

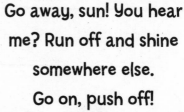

But the sun was
too far away to
hear. It just went
on shining.

Chapter Two

Out in the farmyard the animals looked up at the sun and sighed.

So they all put their hats on, except for Egbert the greedy goat who had already eaten his...

and Pintsize who thought pigs looked
silly in hats. But then Pintsize never did
what he was told.

Down at the pond, Upside and Down, the two white ducks that no one could tell apart, had their heads stuck in the mud because there was hardly any water left in the pond.

Albertine sat still as a statue on her island, shading her goslings under her great white wings.

"When's it going to rain, Mom?" they peeped.

"Sometime," she said, and she settled down to sleep because it was the wisest thing to do and Albertine was the wisest goose that ever lived (and everyone knew it, including Albertine).

So, thirsty and dusty and itchy, the animals trooped down to ask her advice, all except Mossop, the cat with the one and single eye, who was fast asleep on his tractor seat.

Hey, Albertine, what are we going to do?

A cow needs water.

Eighty bottles a day, and there's not much left.

said Diana the silly sheep.

"What about you?" said Jigger, the almost-always-sensible sheepdog.

Frederick looked up at the buzzards and larks and swifts and swallows. "If only I could fly like them. Must be cool up there," he sighed.

And little Pintsize looked up too and thought just the same thing.

"You've got wings," said Egbert.
"Use them."

Oh! He's a bit touchy.

They're for crowing with, you stupid goat!

"Now, now," said Captain. "We're quarrelling again." And he called out to Albertine, "What'll we do, Albertine? The Sun is making us all nasty and mean."

Oh dear!

So that's what they all did—Captain in the darkest corner of his stable,

Jigger under the rhubarb leaves in the vegetable patch,

Auntie Grace and Primrose side by side under the great ash tree,

Egbert behind a pile of paper bags in the barn so he could be near his lunch,

and Diana right in the middle of the sunniest field because she was very, very silly!

Frederick went wherever his speckled hens did—and because they all went in different directions, he found that very difficult!

While Peggoty and her little pigs, including Pintsize, crawled into a patch of nettles and lay still. Soon all the animals were fast asleep…

…except Pintsize who wasn't at all sleepy.

Chapter Three

Of all Peggoty's little pigs, Pintsize was definitely the naughtiest. Say "do this" and he'd do that. Say "come here", and he'd go there. It was just the way he was. Some children are like that.

He waited until Peggoty was snoring,

 then tiptoed through the farmyard

and down the lane,

 looking for really interesting things to do.

He hadn't gone far when he saw old
Farmer Rafferty leaning on a gatepost
and talking to the next-door farmer.
Both of them were gazing up at the sky.

Cows are lying down.
Sure sign of rain.
It's coming—I can smell it.

Farmer Rafferty shook his head as he
squinted at the sun.

And pigs might fly!

he said, and
he laughed like a drain.

Pintsize pricked up his ears, (which isn't easy for a little pig).

Pigs can fly?

I never knew that.

I'm a pig, so that means I can fly. I can fly! I can fly!

And he jumped up and down
in wild excitement.

Boing!
Boing!

Flying was not nearly as easy as it looked. Pintsize stood up on his back hooves and flapped his front ones—hooves, he thought, would do just as well as wings.

But however hard he flapped (and flapping hooves is *not* easy) and however much he jumped up and down, he somehow never managed to take off. But Pintsize was not a giving-up sort of pig. He sat down and thought about it.

Nothing's ever easy at first. I mean, it took me days before I could walk. What was it Mama said to me? Practice makes perfect.

He was out in the meadow, practicing his hoof-flapping, when a crow spotted him and landed beside him.

What are you up to, little piggy thing?

I'm learning to fly.

We've got a silly one here!

The crow cackled and flew off to
tell his friends, then they all cawed
together until they got sore throats—
which served them right.

Suddenly Pintsize had an idea.

Upside and Down,
they can fly.
I've seen them.
They'll teach me.

And he trotted off to the muddy pond.
"Upside! Down!" he squealed, but they
couldn't hear him, not with their heads
in the mud.

In the end he got a long stick and poked
Upside
in his
down,

and Down
somewhere
else!

They were not at all pleased.

"What, like this?" they quacked. And they took off and looped a loop.

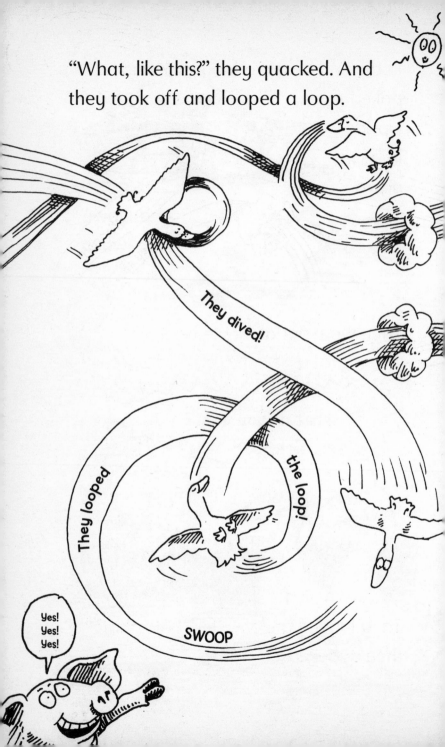

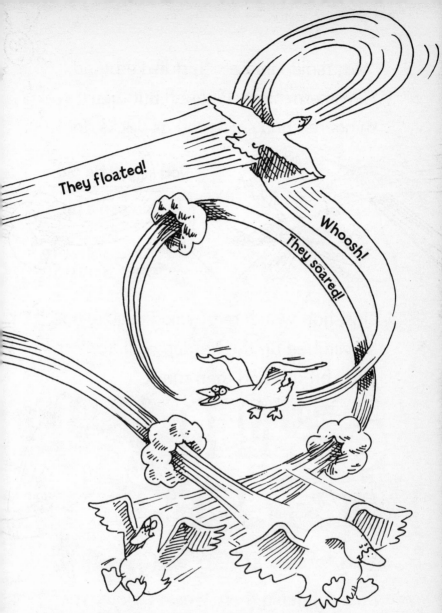

They floated!

Whoosh!

They soared!

They landed quite puffed. "Like that?" they quacked.

"Yes," said Pintsize. "Just like that.
Please teach me. Please." But they
sniggered and snickered as ducks do.

You silly little pig.

You can't fly.

"Just you watch me," said Pintsize, and
he climbed up the garden wall, took a
deep breath and then ran…

It'll all end
in tears, just
you wait and
see!

until suddenly there was no more wall
to run on…and he was flying through
the air!

For one wonderful moment he was up there with the birds, but then something was pulling him down and

down and he
was turning
over
and
over…

Then he landed

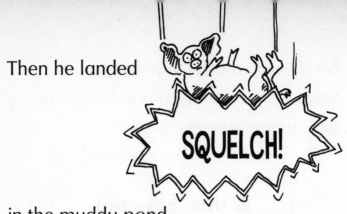

in the muddy pond.

Oh dear, thought Albertine. *I suppose I'd better do something about this.*

So she stood up and honked and honked until all the animals woke up and came running.

It's Pintsize.
He thinks he's a bird.
Look over there.

Pintsize was climbing the ladder (and that's not easy if you're a pig) up on to the haystack.

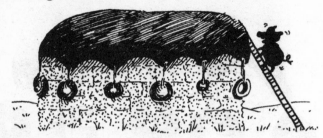

Peggoty closed her eyes, "I'm not looking," she said.

We mustn't let him out of our sight, otherwise he'll hurt himself. Wherever he jumps he's got to have a soft landing. Quick, Jigger! You're the fastest.

Whooooosh.

That's my mom, making the hard decisions.

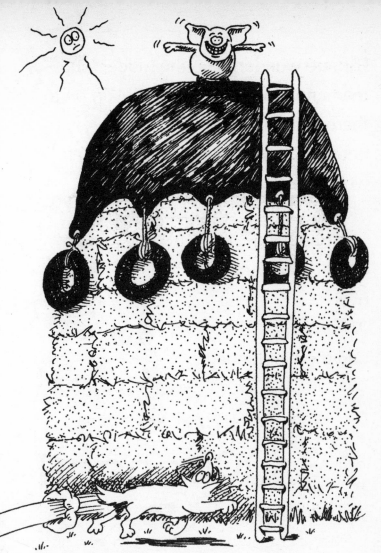

Jigger sprinted across the farmyard
until he was standing right under the
haystack. "Don't jump!" he barked.
"Don't do it..." But Pintsize did it.

For one wonderful
moment he was up
there with the birds,
but then something
was pulling him
 down
      and down
and he was turning
over
   and over,
and then he landed

SQUOOOOOOOF!

on Jigger's back.

Jigger never knew
that little pigs
could be that heavy.
But he knew now.

And very soon they all knew,
because wherever Pintsize went
they had to go, so that whenever he
jumped, one of them was always there
for him to land on.

Every time he jumped, he flew farther
or he thought he did. "I can fly," he'd
squeal. "Pigs can fly."

And it was true—well, sort of.

Pintsize flew as far as a pig ever had
flown, but then he'd drop like a stone
and knock all the air out of poor
Auntie Grace (and that's a lot of air),
or Primrose

or Captain

or Egbert

or Frederick.

But the one he liked landing on most
was Diana, because she was very soft
and very springy and very spongy.

"Thanks, Diana," he'd squeak, and off he'd go again before anyone could catch him.

This can't go on.

You can say that again.

This can't go on.

I've tried everything I can—he just won't listen to me.

Something's got to be done.

Too true, quite right.

But what?

Everyone looked at Albertine to see if she'd had one of her ideas.
And of course she had.

"Don't you worry," she said. "I'll have a word with a friend of mine. I've got friends in high places, you know. Just you keep your eye on Pintsize, all of you."

Drooping in the heat of the day, the animals did as Albertine said and trailed around the farm after Pintsize. They found him teaching his brothers and sisters. Standing up on his back hooves, Pintsize was explaining how a pig flies.

"You just wave these," he said, flapping his front hooves, "and you lift off. Simple when you know how."

And all the little pigs stood up and waved their front hooves.

I'd watch him if I were you, Peggoty.

But I can't look!

While she wasn't looking, a buzzard flew down and landed beside Pintsize.

"Am I ready?" said Pintsize. "Course I'm ready!" And before he knew it, the buzzard had picked him up and was soaring into the sky high above the farm.

"Nice view," said the buzzard.

Pintsize looked down, and wished he hadn't. His stomach started to turn over and he began to feel very sick and very frightened. The animals below him were getting smaller.

And smaller.

Then he couldn't see them any more.

57

"Take me down," he squealed. "Take me down."

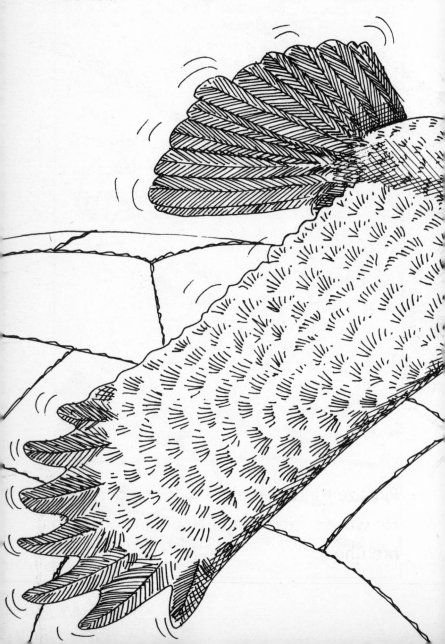

Pintsize tried to scream, but he couldn't.
He was so frightened he couldn't even
breathe…

The farm was coming closer and closer. It was getting bigger and bigger! He was going to crash!

Pintsize closed his eyes.

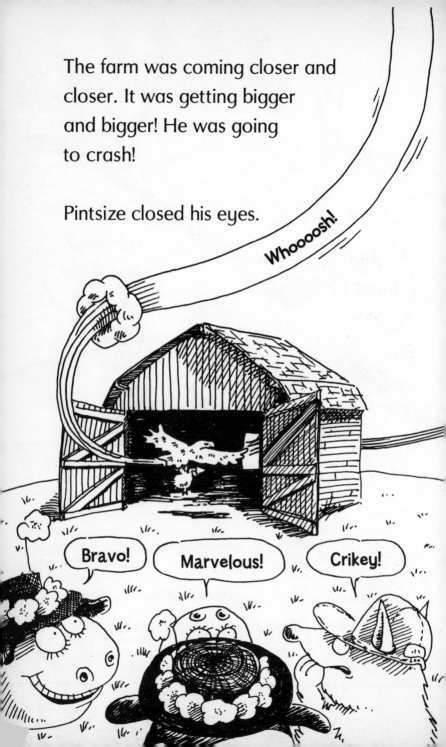

"Not yet," said the buzzard, and as they floated through the silent sky they came to a cloud, a dark cloud. "Don't like the look of that," said the buzzard a bit louder than he should.

Don't much like the look of you either.

Thunder rolled around the sky and the
rain began to fall in great dollops.

"I want to go home," squealed Pintsize.
"I want my mama."

"All right," said the buzzard, "I'll drop
you off."

And he did just that!

Down below, Farmer Rafferty was talking to the next-door farmer again.

"Yippee! Yarroo!" cried old Farmer Rafferty, and he did a sploshy rain dance in a muddy puddle. But if he hadn't been so busy dancing he'd have noticed that it wasn't raining cats and dogs at all—it was raining pigs. And one little pig in particular!

"Yes, Mama," said Pintsize—and he meant it. He snuggled into her and buried his head in the dung so he couldn't hear the thunder.

That evening Jigger saw Albertine as she was having her bath.

"Maybe," said Albertine, and smiled her goosey smile.

Meanwhile...

On his tractor seat, Mossop woke up.

Peggoty put her hooves over Pintsize's ears so he couldn't hear any more.

Oh, for goodness' sake, go back to sleep, Mossop.

yAWN

"If you insist," sulked Mossop, and he yawned hugely as cats do, closed his one and single eye and slept.

The night came down, the moon came up and everyone slept on Mudpuddle Farm.

Jigger's Day Off

There was once a family of all kinds of animals that lived in the farmyard behind the tumbledown barn down on Mudpuddle Farm.

Cock-a-doodle-dooooooo

At first light every morning, Frederick the flame-feathered rooster lifted his eye to the sun and crowed and crowed…

until the light came on in old Farmer Rafferty's bedroom window.

One by one the animals crept out into the dawn and stretched and yawned and scratched themselves; but no one ever spoke a word, not until after breakfast.

"Jigger, my dear," said old Farmer Rafferty, one hazy hot morning in September.

Corn's as high as a house. Fair weather ahead, they say. Time has come for harvest, Jigger. So I won't be needing you all day. It's your day off, my dear. Old Thunder sleeps in his shed all year, now it's his turn to do some work. Got to earn his keep, just like all of us. I'll just go and rub him down.

Wooow! It's my day off!

And off he went.

One day off a year, thought Jigger
the almost-always-sensible sheepdog.
*One day a year when I don't have to
be sensible, when I can do what a dog
likes to do.* And he licked his smiling
lips, and wagged his dusty tail.

Old Thunder lived all by himself in a shed at the end of the yard. No one ever went near him because no one dared.

Pintsize had never seen Old Thunder.
He longed to peek in through
the crack in the doors.

Can't quite see...

Mama,
let me look,
let me look!

he squealed.

Peggoty warned him.

Don't you ever go near
Old Thunder, you hear me?
Not ever.

He's a monster!

said Auntie Grace
the brown cow.

I agree.

And of course
Primrose agreed
with her as she
always did.

As a matter of fact, most of the animals
thought Old Thunder was some sort of
monster.

So when old Farmer Rafferty opened the door of the shed that morning, all the animals went into hiding. Upside and Down turned upside down in terror. Mossop disappeared into a drainpipe. (Everyone was terrified of Old Thunder—except Egbert the greedy goat. He was always too hungry to be frightened.)

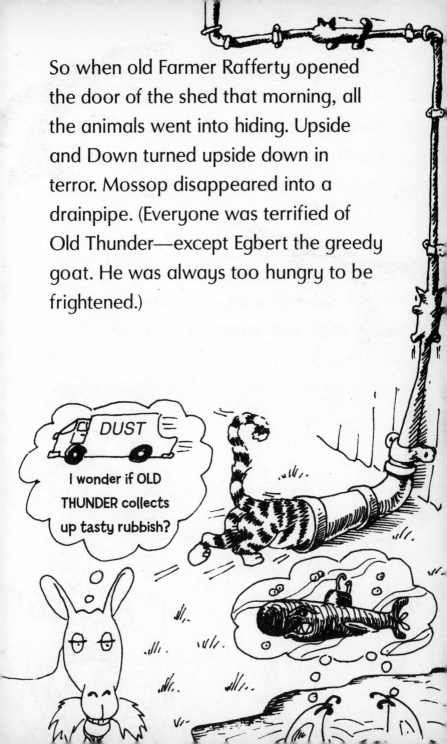

DUST

I wonder if OLD THUNDER collects up tasty rubbish?

Albertine the white goose gathered her goslings around her on her island in the pond and explained everything to them. She wasn't just an intelligent goose, she was a wise mother as well.

At that very and same moment, there was a roar from inside Old Thunder's shed, and he rumbled out into the yard belching smoke and dust. Old Farmer Rafferty sat high and happy on the driver's seat singing his heart out.

"See, children," said Albertine gently. "I told you that's all Old Thunder is, just an old combine harvester."

Without him, there'd be no straw to
lie on in the winter and no corn to eat.
Sometimes, children, I'm quite ashamed of
my friends. I've told them and I've
told them that Old Thunder only
eats corn, but they just do not believe me.

One man went to mow...

Chapter Two

Old Thunder sailed majestically out
through the gate and into the corn field
beyond, his great cutters turning like
the wheels of a giant paddle steamer.
"One man went to mow, went to mow
a meadow," sang old Farmer Rafferty
in his crusty, croaky kind of voice.

went to mow a meadow, one man and his dog (woof! woof!)

went to mow a meadow...

And, behind him, Jigger, the almost-
always-sensible sheepdog, slunk
through the gate and lay down in the
cut corn, his nose on the ground
in between his paws.

He smelt something,

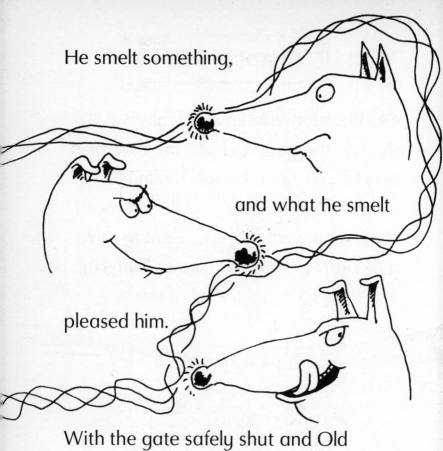

and what he smelt

pleased him.

With the gate safely shut and Old
Thunder roaring around the field,
the animals at last crept out of their
hiding places and stood watching by
the gate—all except Mossop who had
fallen asleep in his drain.

ZZZZZZZZz!

"What's Jigger up to?" asked Diana the silly sheep, who always asked questions but never knew any answers.

Around and around the field went Old Thunder, churning out the straw behind him in long and golden rows. Around and around the field went Jigger, slinking low to the ground.

And every now and then he would stop and stare at the square of standing corn, and every time he stopped, the square was a little bit smaller.

"We shouldn't be standing around in the sunshine," said Captain.

Best go inside. Those flies'll be at us soon.

So they did. Except for Egbert the goat who was busy chewing off the paint from the iron-barred gate.

At eleven o'clock Old Thunder

stopped,

GRUNK!

shuddered,

RIBBLE!

coughed

SPLUT!

and was silent. The birds sang once
more in the bushes.

Ever so carefully, for he
was stiff in his knees,
old Farmer Rafferty
climbed down from
his seat and sat down
to rest in the shade.

It was time for his morning milk. He *always* had it at eleven o'clock no matter where, no matter what.

"I'm making sure Old Thunder doesn't miss anything," said Jigger, but he never took his eyes off the standing corn.

And old Farmer Rafferty laughed because he knew better.

Chapter Three

Around and around the field went Old
Thunder again, churning out the straw
behind him in long and golden rows.
Around and around the field went
Jigger, slinking low to the ground and
every now and then he would stop
and stare at the square of standing
corn that grew smaller all the while
as Old Thunder ate it up.

Albertine was passing the gate with her three yellow goslings peeping behind her. "What's Jigger up to?" they peeped.

"Never you mind," said Albertine, hurrying them on. "Jigger's not himself today, he never is on his day off. This is the one day of the year he's not sensible, and I don't want you to watch."

"Only mad dogs go out in the midday sun," grumbled Egbert the goat, who had finished eating the paint on the gate.

"Mad dogs and goats," said Albertine, but quietly, so that Egbert would not hear. She never liked to upset anyone.

I like a bit of lead-free paint!

At one o'clock Old Thunder stopped again, shuddered, coughed and was silent. The birds sang once more in the bushes.

Ever so carefully, old Farmer Rafferty climbed down from his seat and sat down to eat his lunch in the shade—sandwiches and pickles.

He offered some to Jigger for he knew Jigger was partial to sandwiches. But Jigger was not interested in sandwiches—not today—he had his eye on the golden square of standing corn.

No thanks, can't stop for lunch.

Around and around the field went
Old Thunder again,

churning out the straw behind him

in long and golden rows.

Around and around the field

went Jigger, slinking low

to the ground.

Captain plodded slowly down to the pond for a drink. "Egbert," he said, "is Jigger still out there in this heat?"

"Must be mad, that dog," said Egbert. "Hasn't stopped all day. Around and around and around he goes—makes you dizzy just to look at him. Dunno why he bothers—he never catches anything."

Tastes good, does it, that gatepost?

Bit old!

At four o'clock Old Thunder stopped again, shuddered, coughed and was silent. The birds sang once more in the bushes. Ever so carefully old Farmer Rafferty climbed down from his seat and walked off back toward the farmhouse to fetch his supper.

"Not much more to do," he said as he went. "Got 'em well and truly bottled up, have you, my dear? You'll never get 'em, Jigger, you never do."

But Jigger was not listening to old Farmer Rafferty. He lay with his chin on his paws, his ears pricked forward toward the corn, his nose twitching.

Rabbits and hares, his nose told him,
rats and mice, moles and voles,
pheasants and partridges, beetles
and bugs.

He could hear them all rustling and bustling and squeaking and squealing in the little golden square of standing corn that was left.

Sooner or later he knew they would
have to make a run for it.

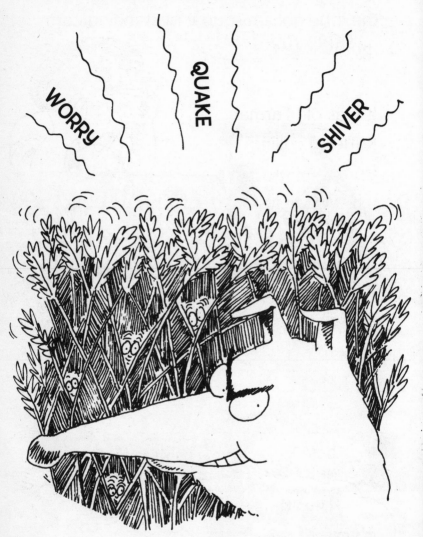

And he'd be waiting.

Chapter Four

Jigger, my dear!

It was old Farmer
Rafferty calling
from the house and
whistling for him.

"Jigger! Come, boy, come, boy! I know
it's your day off, but the sheep have
broken out in Back Meadow.
Come, boy, come, boy!"

I won't!
It's my one day off.
I'll be jiggered
if I'll go!

"Jigger! Jigger!" Old Farmer Rafferty was using his nasty, raspy voice.

You come here, Jigger, else there'll be trouble.

If I go now, I'll have wasted my whole day. There'll be nothing left in that corn for me to chase when I get back.

And then he had an idea.

WOOF!

BARK!

Jigger's barking brought all the animals
running,

waddling...

and flying
to the gate.

"Bring 'em all out into the field,
Captain," he called out. The animals all
looked at each other nervously.

Don't worry.
Old Thunder's
fast asleep.
He's been working
hard.

And so they all went out into the field,
all except Diana the silly sheep who
refused to go anywhere near
Old Thunder, whether he was asleep
or not. Jigger quickly explained
everything to Captain. And he went
off toward the farmhouse.

In no time at all, Captain had them all
organized and ready.

Nothing must leave the
standing corn. Jigger says
that we're to chase it back
if anything comes out.

So Peggoty and
her little pigs,

Including Pintsize!

were sent to guard the north side of the
golden square of standing corn, along
with Egbert.

I'd rather be
eating on old
shoe box

Primrose and Auntie Grace went off to guard the south side with Albertine and her goslings.

Captain himself stayed to guard the east side with Frederick the rooster.

And Mossop,
the cat with
the one and
single eye,
was sent off
to guard the
west side.

Wish it was my day off too!

Now you won't go to sleep, will you?

Course not!
What makes you
think I'd do a
thing like that?

So on three sides of the golden
square of standing corn, the animals
kept watch.

But for Mossop it was all too much.
The sun was hot

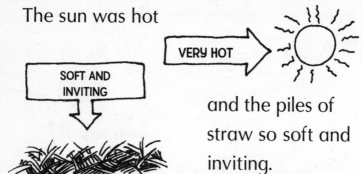

VERY HOT

SOFT AND INVITING

and the piles of
straw so soft and
inviting.

He lay down,

closed his one

and single eye

and

quite forgot what he was there for.

Chapter Five

Now's our chance.

Go for it!

No time to pack.

Quick, while he's asleep.

Mossop snored as he slept, and inside the golden square of corn they heard him and saw him and took their chance.

One by one the little creatures of the cornfield left their hiding places. In one long line they left—westwards...

Rabbits first, then mice and rats,

and moles and voles, and pheasant and partridges,

123

They tiptoed past the snoring cat and out across the open field until they reached the safety of the bushes, where they vanished.

Chapter Six

Not long after this, Jigger came racing back through the gate.

Didn't let anything escape, did you?

Not a one. Good job we did for you, Jigger, good job.

And all the animals hurried back to the farmyard just in case Old Thunder woke up again—all of them except Mossop, who still lay fast asleep in a pile of straw.

"Just this last little square to finish, Jigger," said old Farmer Rafferty after he'd had his supper. "Be finished by sundown, in spite of those darned sheep."

But Jigger was not listening.
He had other things on his mind.
As Old Thunder started up again he
was ready and waiting for the first of
the little creatures to break out of their
hiding place.

Around and around the field went Old Thunder for the last time,

slinking low to the ground.

Jigger for the last time,

churning out straw behind him in long and golden rows. Around and around the field went

By the time the sun set behind the tumbledown barn, not a stalk of corn was left standing. And nothing had come out, no rabbit, no rat, no mouse, no vole, no mole, no pheasant, no partridge, no beetle, and no bug.

Nothing.

"Well, I'll be jiggered," said Jigger.

I don't believe it!

I just don't believe it!

I could have sworn there were hundreds of them in that corn. I could smell 'em. I could hear 'em.

"It's the sun, Jigger," said Mossop, who had just woken up. "Does strange things to you."

Too much sun and you can see things that aren't there,

so I suppose you can hear things that aren't there too.

I suppose you can even smell things when they're not there.

I can tell you, Jigger, nothing came past me when I was on guard. Well, they wouldn't dare, would they?

And he yawned hugely as cats do.

Jigger looked at Mossop sideways and wondered.

"Had a good day off, Jigger, my dear?" old Farmer Rafferty shouted as he passed by high up on Old Thunder.

And old Farmer Rafferty laughed and laughed, until the laughter turned into a song once again.

one man and his dog (woof! woof!) went to mow...
It's been a long day. Don't know about you, Jigger, but I'm just about ready for bed.
Tee hee!

And the night came down and the moon came up and everyone slept on Mudpuddle Farm.

Join the fun on
Mudpuddle Farm

Have you got them all?

Martians at Mudpuddle Farm

Have Martians landed on Mudpuddle Farm?
Farmer Rafferty seems to think so! It looks like an
alien invasion, and in a situation like that there's
only one animal to turn to—Albertine, the
smartest goose in the world...

Mum's the Word

Something strange is going on—instead of grumbling,
Egbert the goat is singing and dancing! And he's even
greedier than usual. But why doesn't Farmer Rafferty
complain when Egbert eats all his carrots?
As always, Albertine has an idea...

michael morpurgo

Mudpuddle Farm

cock-a-poodle-do

illustrated by shoo Rayner

Mossop's Last Chance

Mossop the old farm cat likes to sleep—and not much else! So when Farmer Rafferty tells him to catch twenty-six mice by sunset all the animals have to pull together to give Mossop one last chance. . .

Albertine, Goose Queen

A fox is on the loose, and all the animals except Albertine the goose have hidden themselves inside. Albertine is safe on her island in the pond—at least so she thinks, until the fox starts swimming toward her. . .

michael morpurgo
Mudpuddle Farm

Hee-Haw Hooray!

illustrated by
Shoo Rayner

Nothing to Worry About

There's a storm in the air, and all the animals
are worried, but old Farmer Rafferty
doesn't realize anything is wrong.
Can the animals warn him in time?

Hunky-Dory

A funny new creature arrives and the
animals soon make friends. Problem is, the
latest addition to the farm doesn't actually
belong there! It looks like it's time
to say a sad goodbye—although Albertine
the goose might just have a clever idea. . .